THE Trouble WITH CHICKENS

A J.J. Tully Mystery

DOREEN CRONIN

illustrated by

KEVIN CORNELL

BALZER + BRAY
An Imprint of HarperCollins *Publishers*

THE Trouble WITH CHICKENS

A J.J. Tully Mystery

Balzer + Bray is an imprint of HarperCollins Publishers.

The Trouble with Chickens
Text copyright © 2011 by Doreen Cronin
Illustrations copyright © 2011 by Kevin Cornell

Library of Congress Cataloging-in-Publication Data
Cronin, Doreen.
    The trouble with chickens : a J.J. Tully mystery / Doreen Cronin ; illustrated by
Kevin Cornell. — 1st ed.
        p.   cm.
    Summary: A hard-bitten former search-and-rescue dog helps solve a complicated
missing-chicken case.
    ISBN 978-0-06-121532-2 (trade bdg.) — ISBN 978-0-06-121533-9 (lib. bdg.)
    [1. Dogs—Fiction. 2. Chickens—Fiction. 3. Humorous stories. 4. Mystery and
detective stories.] I. Cornell, Kevin, ill. II. Title.
PZ7.C88135Tr 2011   2009031213
[Fic]—dc22   CIP
                                                                    AC

Typography by Carla Weise
11 12 13 14 15 CG/RRDC 10 9 8 7 6 5 4 3 2 1
❖
First Edition

For Lillian,
John, Vince,
and Marge
—D.C.

For Kim, who
holds my hand
—K.C.

CONTENTS

Chicken Breath

It was a hot, sunny day when I met that crazy chicken.

So hot that sometimes I think the whole thing may have been a mirage.

But mirages don't have chicken breath, mister.

She was a short, tired-looking bird with a funny red comb on her head.

It looked about as useful to her as a spoon is to a snake.

Her eyes were tiny and black, and set so close to each other they practically touched.

I'd be surprised if the right eye could report back seeing anything other than the left eye.

Chickens make me nervous.

Can't keep 'em quiet.

We stared at each other for an awkward moment.

I nodded to tell her to move on.

She picked up her left foot carefully, not sure whether she should back out of my sweltering doghouse.

As her foot hung in midair, she lowered her pointy white head and very deliberately said . . . nothing.

A phone rang.

A car backfired.

A blender roared.

And that crazy chicken didn't blink.

She was one tough bird.

Introductions

My name's Jonathan. Jonathan Joseph Tully. J.J. for short.

I spent seven years as a search-and-rescue dog.

The quiet life in the country where Barb, my trainer, lived was my reward for all those years of service.

Some reward.

I could track the six-day-old scent of a lost hiker and pull a fat guy out from under a pile of rubble, but I couldn't get that crazy chicken out of my yard.

Her name was Millicent.

I called her Moosh, just because it was easier to say and it seemed to annoy her.

She had two little puffy chicks with her.

She called them Little Boo and Peep.

I called them Dirt and Sugar, for no particular reason.

Moosh had got the word that I knew how to solve problems.

Boy, did that chicken have problems.

"I'll pay you in chicken feed," said Moosh.

That was the chicken's first problem.

I don't work for feed.

"No dice," I replied.

Dirt and Sugar were bathing in my water bowl.

"I'll pay you in feathers."

That was the chicken's second problem.

"I already got a pillow," I grumbled.

Dirt and Sugar were playing in my food bowl.

Crazy chicks.

I was losing patience.

"I'll work for a cheeseburger. Take it or leave it."

Moosh's tiny chicken head cast a huge, pointy shadow against the side of my weather-beaten

doghouse. She took a step away from me, turn-ing her head to glance at Dirt and Sugar. Those two feather balls jumped out of my water bowl and rolled around in the grass. They looked like they didn't have a care in the world, but their mom sure did.

A passing cloud offered some uncertain shade from the sun.

Moosh's big, pointy chicken shadow finally moved.

"Done," said Moosh.

"Well done," I cracked.

I thought she smiled, but it's tough to tell with a beak.

3

Chicken Missing

Moosh paced back and forth.

Dirt and Sugar followed behind her.

As Moosh took a step forward, Sugar fell into line right behind her. I expected Dirt to do the same. For some reason, she waited two beats, then got into line.

Dirt left enough space in between herself and Sugar to park a squirrel.

I'm no chicken expert, but something wasn't right.

"Who's missing?" I asked Moosh.

The truth was somewhere between her brain and her beak.

I wasn't sure it would survive the trip.

"Spill it, Moosh," I grunted.

She was getting on my nerves.

Dirt and Sugar stepped out from behind their mother.

They were half yellow, half white—like fuzzy popcorn kernels with feet. They were new enough to this world to be spitting up eggshell. Their eyes were wide and young, and close-set like their mother's.

Sugar cocked her head, stepped out from behind her popcorn sister, and motioned with one tiny wingette for Dirt to stay behind. A ladybug flew into the doghouse and crawled across the floor, oblivious to the chicken tension building in the room.

I growled.

Sugar peeped.

I growled again.

Sugar took a step closer, bracing herself against the water bowl.

"Poppy and Sweetie are missing," she whispered.

She may have looked fluffy and new, but this chick had already learned that life outside the shell was not all it was cracked up to be.

Poppy and Sweetie

Poppy and Sweetie.

Their names annoyed me too.

But it wasn't time for more nicknames.

Nicknames are only cute when your mother knows where you are.

I had Dirt and Sugar take me to the last place they saw Poppy and Sweetie. It was just outside the chicken coop.

I told the fluffy family to stand still. I didn't have any of Poppy's or Sweetie's belongings to sniff, but I had their siblings.

Close enough.

I had no idea how hard it might be to track the scent if I found it. On the job we call it "probability of detection," POD for short. With no personal effects to sniff and no experience tracking poultry, the probability of detection in this case was low—very low. But now was not the time to burden a chicken mother's heart with a low POD.

There's an easy way to do a search and a hard way.

The easy way is early in the evening with a cool breeze and a steady partner.

The hard way is high noon with a crazy chicken clucking in your ear and two feather balls riding your tail.

This search was gonna go the hard way.

I had to give it to Moosh straight.

"Humans have a knack for finding themselves in places where they don't belong—dark woods, cold snow, and deep canyons. Lucky for them, they stink. But I don't know from chickens—so don't get your hopes up."

Moosh took a deep breath. She knew the score. In the harsh sunlight her comb had lost its bright red luster.

It was Fourth of July weekend, and the air was heavy. I got down as low as I could. The earth will hold on to your smelly secrets for a long, long time. And it will give them up to any dog who comes sniffing. Problem is, it gives up all its secrets at once. You have to be able to sniff through them to find the one you need. Bare feet. Barbecue sauce. Blueberries. It didn't take long to pick up what I thought was a chicken trail.

I followed it around the edge of the yard, under a pile of rotting wood, past the barn, and then across the open field.

For all I knew, it could have been a chicken sandwich.

Then something hit me in the eye. Hard.

I stopped in my tracks.

Moosh, Dirt, and Sugar were right behind me.

When I looked up, I got hit again.

It was rain. Hard rain.

The kind of rain that makes grown men wear funny boots.

I called off the search.

Sugar was in my face.

"Listen, mutt, my brother and sister are missing, and you're worried about getting wet?"

She was so close to me, I could have bitten her in half.

"Get lost," I mumbled.

"Make like a sponge, mister."

I had to hand it to Sugar—she was as tough as her mother.

Chicken Scratch

The sky turned from gray to green to black.

If the rain hadn't already washed off the scents of Poppy and Sweetie, it seemed the wind would have blown it away.

After a short stroll in the hard rain, I decided to get back to my warm bed.

I had had enough of this little chicken adventure.

It was time for a nap, after all.

The trouble with doghouses is they don't have doors.

Moosh, Dirt, and Sugar were just a few minutes behind me.

"You smell like wet dog," said Sugar.

"I am a wet dog," I grumbled.

"Is this the 'search' part or the 'rescue' part?" asked Sugar.

She reminded me of a splinter I'd had

once—it bothered me, and I was in a much better mood when it was gone.

Before I could answer her, Moosh waved a note in front of me.

"I found it in the chicken coop," cried Moosh.

I have your peeps. It behooves you to rendezvous. Twilight. Your place.

I tried to grab the note out of Moosh's beak.

That thing was sharper than it looked.

I gave up my hold on the note.

Two things were clear: Whoever had left that note had fast feet and a head full of big words.

Chicken Tears

Moosh paced back and forth.

Sugar and Dirt followed behind her in the same oddly spaced line as before.

I stood in front of Moosh and brought her little chicken parade to a halt.

Sometimes your gut can tell you more than your nose. This was one of those times.

I could see from the look in her eyes that Moosh was thinking about trying to get past me.

I bared my teeth and moved in closer.

That changed her mind.

I've never backed down from a staring contest in my life, but her eyes were so tiny and close-set, it was making me cross-eyed.

I was breathing in what she was breathing out.

Her left foot was bouncing up and down, like she was standing on a hot plate.

She looked down at the note, then she looked down at Dirt and Sugar. When she finally looked up at me, her eyes were filled with tears.

I'm no stranger to tears.

The sad truth about search-and-rescue work is that there isn't always a rescue.

So I'd seen plenty of tears before.

But I had never seen chicken tears.

I hope I never see them again.

Moosh's tears finally got the best of her. Her beak began to quiver.

The note fell to the floor.

I had what I needed.

I didn't want to *hold* her precious note, anyway.

I wanted to *sniff* it.

Sure enough, it reeked of one thing—the same chicken scent I had been following before the storm.

The trail was right under my nose.

Inside Job

Behoove.

Rendezvous.

Twilight.

I've been lowered from a helicopter, strapped to a snowmobile, and flown first-class to France to find a backcountry skier lost in the Alps.

Not once did anyone find it necessary to use the word *behoove*.

My bet was that a chicken the size of a golf ball wouldn't find it necessary either. That note might have been covered in Poppy's and Sweetie's scents, but I was sure it wasn't covered in their words.

Behoove.
Rendezvous.
Twilight.

They were "inside" words. Words you only learn inside, where there are things like comfortable chairs and fresh lemonade.

Out here, with the chickens and the dogs, we don't *behoove*.

I don't have a problem with big words.

But there's a time and a place for them. A muddy note in a chicken coop didn't seem like the right place.

Outside, the rain had gone from a storm to a standstill.

I had been so busy thinking about that note that I hadn't noticed the quiet.

There wasn't enough breeze to ruffle a feather.

Moosh was staring at the note. I watched her eyes scan the page over and over.

"What does it mean?" asked Moosh.

I wasn't sure who she was asking.

Sugar spoke before I could.

"It means we need to be in the chicken coop by six thirty."

Sugar's head wasn't filled with feathers, that's for sure.

I was going to have to keep my eye on her.

Right after my nap.

"Wake me up at six twenty-five."

Detour

Our shadows were long and thin as we headed over to the chicken coop for our rendezvous.

Dirt and Sugar were covered in mud and wet grass and napping in my empty food bowl.

It looked like an Easter basket gone horribly wrong.

"It's time, it's time," Moosh clucked. "We have to get to the chicken coop. C'mon, c'mon."

"Go on ahead, Moosh. I'm gonna keep an eye out from here."

I had a hunch I should stay outside the coop.

I had a hunch once about a roast-beef sandwich I found in an alley in Detroit. It didn't smell quite right, but I was hungry. I ignored the hunch and ate the sandwich. I woke up three days later with an IV needle jammed into my front paw courtesy of the Detroit Animal Clinic.

That was one bad sandwich.

The same little voice I had ignored in Detroit was now telling me to stay outside.

I stayed outside.

Moosh was not completely convinced that I wasn't gonna ditch her as soon as her back was turned.

I wasn't completely convinced myself.

"Go on, Moosh," I repeated.

Dirt gave her mom a little tug and led her into the coop.

Sugar stuck around just long enough to throw me a dirty look.

I threw it back.

I was walking away to find decent cover when the scent hit me square in the face.

I may have actually tripped over it.

It was the same scent that was all over the note.

The rain hadn't washed away the chicken scent after all.

But it didn't lead to the chicken coop.

It led to the house.

Moosh shot her head out of the coop. "It's six thirty-three—where are they? Where are they? Where are they?"

I had to put my paw over her face to can the clucking.

Once again, I noted her sharp beak.

"Moosh, we got a new development here."

I held her beak closed with my paw and explained the scent trail leading right up to the house.

"Mmmrrrnneee," she mumbled.

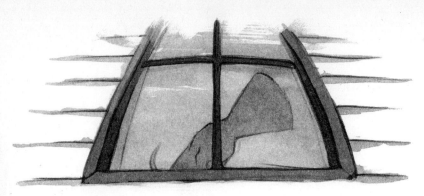

I let go of her beak.

"It can't be," she said again.

"Noses don't lie," I answered.

"But what about the note?" she asked.

"Decoy," I grumbled.

"But it doesn't make any sense . . ."

Before she could finish her sentence, a dark shadow appeared in the window. The shades were drawn, but you could clearly make out the silhouette.

There was no mistaking that silhouette.

Vince the Funnel.

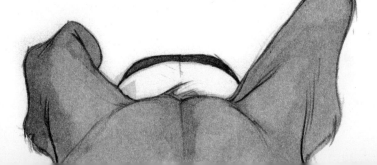

Vince the Funnel

Vince was thirty-seven pounds of shiny brown mutt.

He had a long, skinny build, beady eyes, and a giant white funnel around his neck.

He looked like a cross between a dachshund and a lamp.

We had met the very first day I'd arrived here at Barb's country house.

I had nodded at him that morning almost two weeks earlier.

It was a gesture of goodwill.

He didn't nod back.

Fine by me.

I didn't need any new friends.

I could, however, have used a lamp.

Up to now, I had never exchanged a word with Vince the Funnel.

He spent his time inside.

I spent my time outside.

I preferred to keep things that way.

But a deal is a deal, even if you make it with a crazy chicken.

What little I did know about Vince, I knew from a distance and from the grapevine.

I knew that a dog walker came by every day to take him outside.

And I'd heard he was a little off his rocker.

While I was taking an inventory of what I knew about Vince, Moosh kept herself busy by losing her mind.

"Vince the Funnel has my chicks!" screamed Moosh.

She was running around like a chicken without a head.

Dirt and Sugar were frozen in place, their fuzzy little chicken brains on overdrive.

Inside dog.

Inside words.

It was all beginning to make sense.

Before I could think any further, my stomach rumbled.

I was starving.

I should have asked for that cheeseburger up front.

Funnel Vision

Oh, *how Barb loves losers,* I thought, watching J.J. the Hero Dog march around the yard with Chicken Mom on his tail and his face to the ground. Only an arrogant search-and-rescue dog could undergo years of training but not recognize a simple trap when it's right under his nose. Makes me laugh out loud. But Hero Dog isn't like Barb's usual rejects—the orphan baby birds, the mangy stray cats. I'll have to figure out his weak spot when I have

him up close and personal.

"Welcome to my school, Hero Dog," I muttered. "No medals and no parades here, pretty boy. Just my house, my yard, and my rules. Soon you'll meet one brilliant alpha dog who doesn't like company."

I chuckled to myself and then leaped off the table in front of the window. On the way down, the funnel caught the edge of the lamp, and it crashed to the floor.

The lamp shattered.

A bulb burst.

Two tiny chickens squawked.

I couldn't have planned it better myself.

Why Me?

Vince's shadow had disappeared, and the commotion made it clear that it no longer *behooved* us to *rendezvous*.

I didn't have to turn around to tell what was going on behind me.

Sugar was coming at me as fast as those freaky little chickadee legs would take her.

She hadn't just inherited her mother's eyes, she'd inherited her mother's crazy.

"You're going in, right?" asked Sugar.

I rolled my eyes.

"I'm not going anywhere until I have more information."

"You have all the information you need. Poppy and Sweetie are in the house. You said so yourself."

"No, I said the trail leads to the house. Are you listening to me? Do you even have ears?"

For the first time that day, I bothered to check to make sure chickens had ears.

They do.

Sugar looked over at the house. The back steps were just a few yards away.

To the right was an old birdbath.

To the left was a droopy tomato plant.

Barb must have saved all the pretty for the front of the house.

"I'm going in," Sugar chirped.

She was off in a flash with her eyes locked on the doggie door.

In that second I was sure of only one thing: If she went in, she wasn't coming out.

I grabbed her by the scruff of the neck and looked for someplace safe to stash her for a few minutes.

I tossed her up on the birdbath.

"Sit down and keep quiet."

She kicked a pebble at me.

I thought about the small town in the Midwest that had held a parade in my honor after I pulled three tornado victims out from under a mountain of debris. If you had told me then that I'd someday be dodging pebbles tossed by a baby chicken, I would have bitten you.

Hard.

Like I said, I didn't belong here.

I was as out of place in the country as the guy I once pulled out of a snowy cave in his pajamas.

Life is strange, mister.

Come on Down!

The stairs leading up to the back door were steep and narrow.

Each one sagged a little more than the one above it.

The back door was rusty and crooked, with one small window and a floral shade.

I steadied myself on my back paws and then peered in through the strip of glass beneath the bottom of the shade. I could see down a long, dark corridor

with a polished linoleum floor. Off to the right, I could just make out the edge of a refrigerator in an orange kitchen. Straight ahead, at the end of the hallway, was a dark room with a big-screen TV showing a game show. The game-show host was laughing while an energetic woman in a wrinkled green dress was jumping up and down.

It was dizzying.

I had to look away to clear my head.

I looked back down the long, dark corridor.

I could make out the dim, gleaming arc of a giant plastic cone.

Vince was sitting on the couch, but only for a second.

Before I could even get my front paws back down to the top step, he leaped off that couch and charged the back door. Except at the moment that Vince should have been crashing through the doggie door, he was just crashing.

He was trying to get out, but the funnel had other ideas.

That mutt was in the fight of his life—with his own neck.

He lost the fight.

But I have to admit, at that moment he'd have won just a little bit of my respect if it hadn't been for the fact that he spent his entire life drinking out of a toilet bowl.

It was time to pull Sugar off the birdbath.

One problem.

There was nothing in that birdbath but dirty water and a wet note.

Sugar was gone.

I didn't need the note to tell me where she was. She was in the house.

Call it a hunch.

I met up with Moosh and Dirt back at my doghouse and showed them the note.

Three down,
one to go.

I thought Moosh might crack into a million pieces.

"Here are the hard facts—I can't get into that house. Vince will smell me coming a mile away. But we need more information if we're gonna get them out of there."

Dirt was all ears. Moosh was all mouth.

"I can fit through the door. I'll go in," she said.

Her left foot was bouncing up and down again.

That strange tic was really getting on my nerves.

"I've seen you under pressure," I answered. "Bad plan. There's only one of us who can pull this off."

Dirt planted her feet, raised her dark eyes, and stuck out her skinny chest. She looked like a toothpick with a head. She was about to speak when a ladybug flew by.

"Pretty polka dots," she remarked.

Oh, brother.

Rehearsal

Search-and-rescue dogs are a rare breed.

We have to be half strength, half persever-ance, and half obedience.

Do your own math, tough guy—I'm making a point here.

If you don't have the good sense to follow orders, you are about as useful on a search-and-rescue mission as a scoop of vanilla ice cream.

I wasn't sure what Dirt was made of, but I'd

seen her follow Sugar around and do what she was told.

If ever there was going to be a search-and-rescue chicken, she was it.

If ever there was a mutt who could train a rescue chicken, it was me.

I had one hour to teach a baby bird what had taken me and every other working dog I know more than two years of training to learn.

Luckily, we had plenty of chicken feed.

Turns out I'm a natural.

I used a stick in the dirt floor of the doghouse to draw a diagram of what I had seen of the layout of the house. It looked something like this.

I was going to go straight up the front steps and cause a distraction. When Dirt heard Vince barking, she was going to run in through the doggie door and make a mad dash for the couch. The funnel made it impossible for Vince to get into small spaces. Once Dirt was under the couch, she would be safe long enough to catch her breath.

Her mission was to look for any signs of her siblings and then get out.

Dirt was paying close attention.

Moosh did the same.

We went over it a dozen times.

Every time Dirt repeated my instructions back to me, she got a pawful of chicken feed.

Run.

Hide.

Breathe.

Watch.

Run.

I call it RHBWR, but it's hard to pronounce.

We practiced RHBWR for an hour.

Well, an hour in dog time.

Which is seven hours in people time.

Which translates into forty-three hours in chicken time.

It was a long time.

Moosh didn't interfere.

That's when I knew something was up.

Interference was Moosh's middle name.

I was about to send her chick into a strange

house with an angry dog, and she had nothing to say.

I was so busy being search-and-rescue teacher of the year that I didn't realize who the actual student was.

I thought I was training Dirt.

But I had actually trained Moosh.

She stuck around just long enough to learn what she needed to know.

Then she used Dirt to distract me while she snuck off to RHBWR.

I had no idea how long she'd been gone.

All in the Timing

Chicken Mom crashed through the doggie door looking for a fight. For once, I was actually grateful for the funnel. It saved my ears from some nasty pecks.

"Relax, Mom," I said. "They're all here. We've been expecting you." I nodded toward the couch. I couldn't tell the chicks apart unless they opened their mouths, which they did now, peeping like crazy. I told them to keep their mouths shut.

"I'm not leaving here without them," she said.

"I don't want you or your chicks," I said. "I want your big, dumb friend, outside."

"J.J.?" asked Chicken Mom. "What for?"

I got as close to her face as I could.

"What do you care?"

She didn't flinch.

She was one tough bird.

She just wanted her chicks back and wanted out. I had to get her to trust me.

Before I could say another word, I heard Hero Dog coming up the back steps.

"If I were you, Chicken Mom," I warned, "I'd get out of the way."

Covered in Dirt

Vince was going to be on Moosh's tail the moment she got inside.

And she was too big to fit under the couch.

This wasn't a search anymore.

It was a rescue.

Rescue is where I belong.

Sometimes there's a plan, sometimes there's only adrenaline.

Sometimes adrenaline is all you need.

It was just a short sprint over the damp

yard to get to the back door.

The grass was slippery and cool under my feet.

I was off so fast, I couldn't have changed my mind if I'd wanted to.

Dirt held on to my collar as I barreled across the yard, up the steps, and straight through the doggie door.

A bad feeling went through me like a shiver.

The walls were a dingy blur as we slid down the long corridor.

I cleared the couch, but the room was too short.

I dug my nails into the small, flowery carpet.

The rug carried me like a sled.

Dirt was as good as scrambled egg if she slammed into that wall.

I flipped my head back and threw her off.

At that moment, I realized what the bad shiver was all about.

Vince should have been barking the moment Moosh set foot through the door.

But I hadn't heard a bark out of Vince for hours.

It was the last thing I remembered before everything went black.

Dog Day Afternoon

Hero Dog knocked himself out. I hadn't planned on it, but it was a nice touch.

As for the chickens, everything went almost exactly as rehearsed. The smallest one seemed to have second thoughts, but a nudge of plastic cone moved her along.

Hero Dog was exactly where I wanted him, and the chicks didn't have a clue.

Chicken Mom was my only problem.

She was pretty uptight about the whole thing.

I had to buy some time.

"Hey, you." I pointed to one of the chicks. "Run outside and get your Mom a nice chicken-feed snack."

Chicken Mom eyed me suspiciously while the smallest one ran out the doggie door.

"See? Nothing to worry about, Mom. You can leave anytime you like," I lied.

The rain had started up again, with thunder and lightning to boot.

The smallest chick was back with the feed in a flash.

"Have a snack and stay dry," I said.

I put on the TV to sweeten the deal.

Chicken Mom and her brood were warm, dry, and staying put.

Five chickens in here is five too many. I

was looking
forward to the
peace and quiet
that nightfall
would bring.
I'm going to get rid of
all of them and I don't
even have to leave the
house. Unlike our Hero
Dog, I didn't need years
of training—I was born brilliant.

Dog in the Can

I woke up behind bars.

Either something had gone terribly wrong, or I was back in Detroit.

I jumped to my feet and tried to get my bearings.

It was dark outside.

A clock ticked.

A faucet leaked.

Plop.

Tick.

Plop.

Tock.

Plop.

Tick.

I was locked inside a dog crate in the kitchen.

Vince was outside the crate.

Inside dog.

Outside dog.

Interesting twist.

He had a chick on either side, like a set of dusty bookends.

The rest of the flock was behind him.

"It's about time," said one of the bookends.

"Poppy and Sweetie, I presume," I snarled.

My mind was spinning, but my eyes were steady.

I set them on Moosh.

She met my eyes.

I knew there wasn't a single chicken in that room I could trust.

"It was a trick. He used us to lure you . . ." she stammered.

"I'm done with you, Millicent," I interrupted.

She winced when I called her by her real name.

I took my eyes off Moosh and planted them on Vince.

"It doesn't seem like anybody here needs rescuing," I said.

Poppy and Sweetie giggled nervously.

"They got themselves in here; they can get themselves out," answered Vince.

"That's more than I can say for you," added Poppy.

I bared my teeth.

Poppy backed away from the bars.

But he was right.

The door of the cage was locked with a sliding bolt.

I had no idea how I was going to get out.

Moosh gathered up her chicks and left the room without a word.

Vince sauntered over to his water bowl by the refrigerator.

Now that his giant funnel was out of the way, I could see the note hanging on the fridge:

Dog Walker,

Please take Vince to his vet

appointment at 2 P.M. Monday. He will

be getting ear tubes and staying at the
animal hospital. Thank you.
Barb

I was on my way to the vet for ear tubes!

I had to get out of that cage.

I've pulled people out of all kinds of places—
cars, caves, crevices, and sewer pipes.

But not once have I come across a lock.

I needed a plan. But my head still hurt.

Plop.

Tick.

Plop.

Tock.

Plop.

Tick.

I needed a nap.

Encyclopedia Chickannia

"**Y**ou okay?" came a tiny voice.

I saw a pretty pair of wings.

Unless my fairy godmother was a chicken, it was nobody I wanted to talk to.

"You okay?" she repeated.

It was Sugar.

I didn't answer her.

I turned my back and closed my eyes.

When I opened them, the sun was setting.

Sugar was still there.

"Shouldn't you be long gone by now?" I asked.

"Vince said it's safer if we wait until dark," she said.

"Safer for whom?" I asked.

She didn't answer.

I had no idea why I was even talking to her.

But when you're in a cage, you can't be picky about your company.

"How did I get in here?" I asked.

"You jumped over the couch, landed against the wall, and knocked yourself out cold," she answered.

"But how did I get in the cage?" I asked.

"Vince made us line up the recycle bottles and we rolled you in," she said.

Vince wasn't as dumb as he looked.

We didn't speak for a minute.

Then I continued my line of questioning.

"Who grabbed you off the birdbath?" I asked.

"I got myself off the birdbath."

"How?" I asked. "Chickens can't fly."

"Sure we can. Not very well, but enough to get off a birdbath."

"I don't believe you."

"You should read more," she said.

I turned my back on her again.

"Maybe if you read a book, you would know that we actually can fly short distances. Sometimes we fly to rendezvous with other chickens, usually to flee danger."

My ears perked up.

"You don't say. . . ."

She came right up to the cage.

"Sometimes it behooves breeders to have our wings clipped."

"You don't say. . . ."

For all I cared, she had just recited the small print off the bottom of a mattress tag.

All I had heard from her rant was "Blah, blah, blah, *rendezvous*, blah, blah, blah, *behoove*."

Show and Tell

"**Y**ou wrote the notes," I said to Sugar.

Sugar took another step toward the cage, careful not to get too close.

"Did not."

"Did."

"Did not."

"Did."

"Did not."

It was like a game of Ping-Pong.

I hate Ping-Pong.

"Spill it, Sugar," a voice piped up.

Moosh stepped out of the kitchen shadows.

All the color drained from Sugar's face.

She instinctively took a step back from the trouble coming her way.

I had one second to act.

I sucked my breath in through my nose as hard as I could.

Sugar was dragged right between the two bars and stuck to my nose like a stray sock on a freshly dried towel.

I had no idea what I was going to do with her.

It was Moosh's turn to come up to the cage.

I thought she'd come to rescue Sugar.

I was wrong.

"J.J.'s right," she said. "I knew it as soon as I saw the note."

Aha. I knew she knew more than she said she knew when she knew it.

It explained her bouncing left foot.

It wasn't a tap or a tic—it was a tell.

A tell is something people do when they're lying.

In Moosh's case, it was something she did when she knew more than she said she knew when she knew it.

Moosh stuck her beak through the bars.

"I'm waiting," she said.

"I wrote it," Sugar confessed. "I sent Poppy and Sweetie into the house, but I had to make it look like Vince took them."

"Why in the world would you do that?" Moosh asked.

"For the books," Sugar answered.

"What books?" Moosh said. "We don't have any books."

"Look around, Moosh. This house is filled with books," I said.

Moosh's eyes got big and wide.

"Vince said I had to help him get J.J. into the house or he wouldn't let me back in to read the books," Sugar added.

Finally Moosh understood that Sugar had been coming and going to this house for a long time.

"You faked a kidnapping? With Vince the Funnel?"

Moosh raised her voice so high, I thought she might cough up a vocal cord.

"Vince promised me he wouldn't hurt them. He let them watch TV."

Moosh considered this for a second.

"Vince forced you to write those notes?" she said.

"Actually, they were my idea," said Sugar. "I had to make sure you went to J.J. for help."

"That's enough!" a voice interrupted.

Vince had come into the kitchen with Poppy and Sweetie in tow.

"I should have known you'd sing like a bird," he growled at Sugar.

"I am a bird," she chirped.

Vince bared his teeth. "You're lucky you're in that cage."

He turned to me.

"Congratulations, Hero Dog. You figured it

all out." Vince snickered. "But you're still in a cage, and you're still going to the vet to get ear tubes. You can thank your little chicken family for that."

I charged the front door of the cage as hard as I could.

The door didn't budge.

When I got back on my feet, the chickens were gone.

Vince got as close to the cage as the funnel would let him.

"So who rescues the rescue dog?" he asked.

"Don't you think your dog walker is gonna notice that I'm not you?"

"Regular guy is gone for the holiday. His cousin is filling in. Never seen me before," he answered.

"You've got a bigger problem," I added.

"What's that?"

"When Barb gets back, she's gonna know the wrong dog got the tubes," I said.

"Yeah, but she's not gonna care," he said.

"Why's that?"

"She's going to be too upset over the demise of her pet chickens . . . and she's gonna blame you."

Sugar made a very strange noise right before she fainted.

I had forgotten she was still in the cage with me.

So, apparently, had Vince.

"Don't even bother trying to warn them," he sneered. "The doggie door is controlled by the black tag on my collar. They can't get out unless I let them out."

He was still snickering when he left the room.

So that's what that funny black tag on his collar was for.

I thought it was the on/off switch for the lamp.

I needed more information from Sugar.

One good dose of dog breath was all it took to wake her up.

"All this for a book?" I asked.

"It's a really good book," she whispered.

Then she fainted again.

RHBWR

"**T**ell me everything you know. Now," I said when Sugar came to.

Sugar spilled her guts for real this time.

There was still one step left in Vince's plan. As soon as it was dark, they had to help him get his funnel off.

"Vince says when we're done, everyone will know that you're a dupe and he's a dirty double-crosser," she ended.

"Do you have any idea what that means?"

I asked, exasperated.

"None whatsoever," she said.

"It means Vince is a liar and you are in serious trouble."

It was Dirt.

"Where have you been?" I asked.

"Under the couch," Dirt answered.

"Doing what?" I asked her.

"RHBWRing," she said.

"Stop mumbling," I said.

Dirt rolled her eyes.

"Oh, got it," I said.

Moosh's voice arrived in the kitchen before she did.

"I'm not leaving here without Sugar. So let her go, J.J.—she can't help you," she said.

She stopped dead in her tracks.

"Dirt! Where have you been?"

"Under the couch," she said.

"Doing what?" demanded her mother.

"RHBWRing," she answered.

"Stop mumbling," said Moosh.

Dirt let out a heavy sigh.

"Never mind—we're leaving," said Moosh. "I'm sorry for all the trouble, J.J., but I'm getting my family out of here."

"Where are Poppy and Sweetie?" asked Sugar.

She sounded worried.

"I sent them to wake Vince up so we can take off his funnel and get out of here," said Moosh.

Dirt was through the door before Moosh could finish her sentence.

Sugar made that funny sound again, like she was going to pass out.

This time I caught her before she fell over.

"Moosh, that funnel is the only thing between Vince and your chicks," I said. "Once that thing is off, you're doomed. All of you."

Moosh ignored me. "I won't be tricked again," she said. "We're leaving."

"Moosh, you're not listening."

I was getting pretty agitated.

"Vince is not going to let you go."

I shoved Sugar out through the bars to let

Moosh know I was serious.

Dirt was back in a flash, with Poppy and Sweetie behind her.

"Mom, the doggie door is locked. We can't get out."

Moosh looked scared.

"I can take him," she squawked.

"No, you can't," I said.

Dirt took a good look around the kitchen.

The note on the fridge.

The lock on the cage.

The recycle bin full of bottles.

"I have a plan," she said.

Then she grabbed a pencil and paper and drew her own diagram.

Rescue

The sun had set and the kitchen was dark.

The fireworks had begun. They shed just enough light for us to make out our own shadows.

Unlocking the bolt was easy for Moosh. All it took was some jerky movements of her head with her beak in the loop of the bolt.

I have to admit, she's pretty handy with that sharp beak of hers.

I had Poppy, Sweetie, and Dirt in the cage

with me, but we could barely see one another.

I knew that they were counting on me, but it suddenly hit me that I was counting on them, too. It was not a great feeling.

All kinds of things can affect the outcome of a rescue—timing, weather, terrain, fatigue . . . and sometimes just dumb luck. We were counting on everything going just right. That rarely happens with people—I had no idea what the odds were with chickens.

Vince arrived right on time.

About two feet in front of the crate, Moosh stopped him in his tracks.

"I'll take off the funnel. I've got the sharpest beak," she said.

Her voice shook a little, but Vince didn't seem to notice.

"Fine by me," said Vince.

Moosh had to act fast now.

If she hesitated, we were lost.

I had a new appreciation for the pajama guy in the snowy cave, the lost skier in the Alps, and the victims waiting under piles of debris. My heartbeat always pounded with excitement as the rescue got closer . . . theirs was always pounding with fear. It was not the same feeling. I like the rescue beat much better.

"This is harder than it looks," said Moosh, buying herself some time as she worked furiously on Vince's collar instead of the funnel.

"Hurry it up," Vince growled. I said nothing. But silently, I seconded the motion. He sounded like he meant business. Moosh stood her ground and kept on pecking.

"Lower your head," she told him.

Carefully Moosh clipped the infrared tag off Vince's collar and held it in her beak.

Then she dropped it to the floor and quickly kicked it to Sugar.

Wait for it, I told myself.

My heart was pounding.

Vince caught a glimpse of Sugar running toward the crate with the tag.

Wait for it, I told myself.

I held my breath.

While Sugar was running back to the cage,

Dirt, Poppy, and Sweetie ran out the back of the crate between the bars.

Now.

I threw open the unlocked cage door and made just enough room for Vince.

Vince came down hard on his front paws and slid right in headfirst.

It wasn't the linoleum that did him in; it was the empty plastic bottles.

Just one more reason to recycle.

Gingerly, I stepped over his big back paws and out the door.

Dirt did the honors of slamming the door closed.

Moosh slid the lock back into place.

Vince was inside the cage.

I was outside the cage.

Just the way I liked it.

"Great plan," I said to Dirt.

"Great teacher," she replied.

My heart was still pounding.

But it was the rescue beat now.

Inside Out

There was still something I didn't understand.

I turned to Vince.

"Why did you chase me away from here the first time? What about that wrestling match with the doggie door?"

"Big search-and-rescue hero," he snarled. "Dogs like you are easy to read. If you didn't think the chicks were in danger, there wouldn't be any rescue, would there?"

He had a point.

Poppy and Sweetie were next.

"And you've been watching television for two days?"

"We came for the TV, we stayed for the books," said Sweetie.

Couldn't argue with that.

The fireworks were over and it was time to go.

Those little chicks were still in a heap of trouble with their mom, but at least my trouble was over.

"What's wrong with you, anyway?" I asked Vince.

"What do you mean?"

"The giant funnel?"

"Chronic ear infection."

I changed the subject.

"Why did you let Sugar in here in the first place?"

"Can't reach my ears."

"Sorry?"

"She scratches my ears with her beak."

I tried not to laugh.

I still had something on my mind.

"How did you know that Sugar wrote the notes?" I asked Moosh.

She took a deep breath. She was back in my good graces and wanted to stay there.

"Call it mother's instinct," she said.

"You could have told me," I answered.

"You would have walked away," she replied.

"True," I said.

"I was just a worried mom looking for my kids. I did what I had to do."

She was looking me in the eye.

Her left foot was perfectly still.

"All right, Moosh. You and me are square."

I thought she smiled, but again, it's tough to tell with a beak.

Reward

"About that cheeseburger..." I said to Moosh.

"There's no cheeseburger," she said, "but you knew that."

"I guess I did," I replied.

Moosh headed back to the living room and hopped up on the couch.

I watched as Sugar waited a beat, then did the same.

The rest of the brood followed.

They were finally all together, but there

was a huge spot between Moosh and Sugar.

It didn't make any sense.

"That must be one big chicken you're missing," I joked.

Moosh looked right at me.

Sugar motioned for me with her tiny wing.

The spot between Moosh and Sugar was just my size.

It did look kind of comfy up there.

I jumped up on the couch.

Moosh.

Me.

Sugar.

Poppy.

Sweetie.

Dirt.

Sometimes, you find yourself exactly where you belong.

Epilogue

Vince the Funnel got his ear tubes as planned and came back with an even bigger funnel wrapped around his head. Occasionally we hear a crash coming from the house, and we know he still hasn't quite adjusted to it.

I had to give Vince credit, though. He knew exactly how to push my buttons. Smart guy. Can't stand him, but he's a smart guy.

Sugar is teaching the rest of the family to read. We helped ourselves to a few books before we left the house that night. Barb doesn't seem to have noticed.

Sometimes when the chicks gather in the doghouse, I entertain them with tales of rescue from my glory days. It was Dirt who asked me why my rescue days were over. She always catches me off guard, that one. I wasn't ready to tell that story yet. But sooner or later, I'll tell. And if Sugar has her way— and she usually does—I guess it'll be sooner, not later, because Sugar . . . well, that chick will sure go a long way out of her way for a good story.

Coming soon . . .

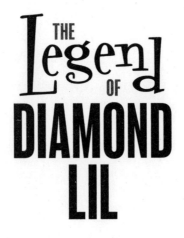

THE
Legend
OF
DIAMOND
LIL